P9-BZB-207

To ISABEL~
WITHLOVE
LIZZY-RENNY.
2000

My Day
in the
Garden

MIELA FORD

My Day in the Garden

PICTURES BY
ANITA LOBEL

Greenwillow Books, New York

Watercolor and gouache paints were used to create the full-color art.
The text type is Seagull Light.

Text copyright © 1999 by Miela Ford
Illustrations copyright © 1999 by Anita Lobel

All rights reserved. No part of this book may be reproduced or utilized in any form
or by any means, electronic or mechanical, including photocopying, recording, or by
any information storage and retrieval system, without permission in writing
from the Publisher, Greenwillow Books, a division of William Morrow & Company, Inc.,
1350 Avenue of the Americas, New York, NY 10019.
www.williammorrow.com
Printed in Singapore by Tien Wah Press
First Edition   10 9 8 7 6 5 4 3 2 1

Library of Congress Cataloging-in-Publication Data
Ford, Miela.
My day in the garden / by Miela Ford ; pictures by Anita Lobel.
p.   cm.
Summary: A young girl and her friends spend the day dressing
up like the insects and animals they find in the garden.
ISBN 0-688-15541-3 (trade).   ISBN 0-688-15542-1 (lib. bdg.)
[1. Insects—Fiction.   2. Animals—Fiction.   3. Gardens—Fiction.
4. Costume—Fiction.]   I. Lobel, Anita, ill.   II. Title.
PZ7.F75322My   1999   [E]—dc21
97-34450   CIP   AC

In memory of my father
—M. F.

For everyone
who makes magic on a rainy day
—A. L.

It's time

to start

the show.

Breakfast with
the morning glories.

Hide-and-seek
with a toad.

Flower-counting
with the butterflies.

Berry-picking
with the birds.

Lunch with
the ladybugs.

Under a tree
for a nap.

Zee zeeeee ze-zoooom.
Crickets sing me to sleep.

Kaw kaw ka-kaw.
Crows wake me up.

I dig with
the worms,

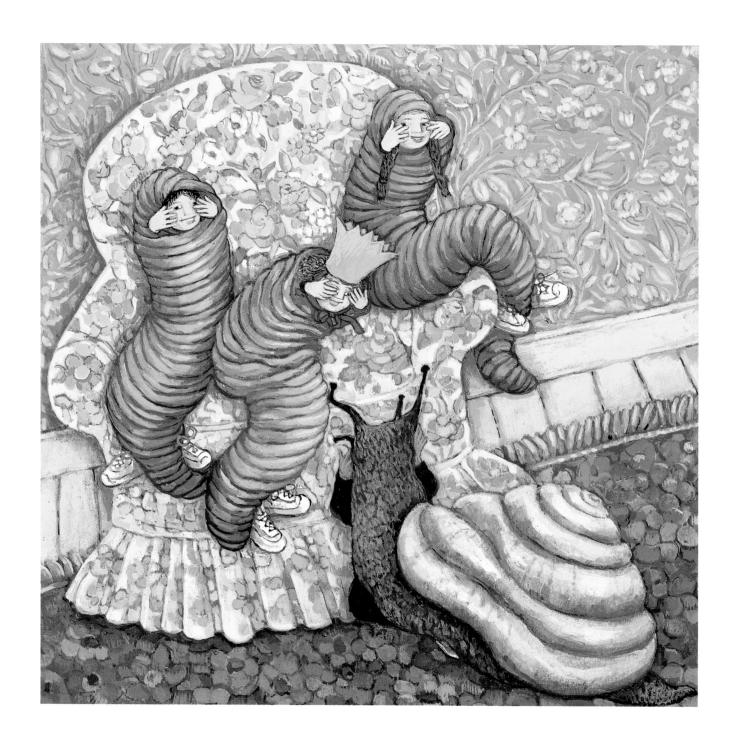

play peek-a-boo
with a snail,

dine with the dragonflies.

Now it's getting dark.

Fireflies come to say good-night.
The curtains close.

Sweet dreams.

Miela Ford grew up in Philadelphia,
where she was born. She graduated
from the Philadelphia College of Art.
The author now lives with her husband
in Rochester, New York, where they love
to watch their garden grow.

Anita Lobel's interest in theater
and costume design inspired her as
she worked on the pictures for this book.
The artist lives in New York City,
where she does not have a garden
but loves to buy cut flowers.